To Jenny —
Happy reading —
Helen Roney Sattler

The Smallest Witch

by Helen Roney Sattler

illustrated by June Goldsborough

ELSEVIER/NELSON BOOKS
New York

Library of Congress Catalog Card Number 81-2202   ISBN 0-525-66747-4
Published in the United States by Elsevier-Dutton Publishing Co., Inc.,
2 Park Avenue, New York, N.Y. 10016.
Printed in the U.S.A.   First edition
10 9 8 7 6 5 4 3 2 1

Dedicated to
my granddaughter,
Branda Lea

The moon was like a bright yellow balloon in the dark sky. Wendy watched as, one by one, the older witches mounted their brooms, gave the magic sign, and took off, their trusty black cats riding tail guard.

It was the most important night of the year to the witches — the night of harvest. All the able-bodied witches who were old enough went out to gather cobwebs. They needed lots and lots of cob-webs to weave their magic spells.

Wendy wished that she could go, too.

"You are not old enough yet," the supervisor told her. "You stay here and help the dispatcher."

So Wendy carefully crossed each name off the list as the dispatcher sent the other witches on their way.

"If I do a really good job this year, they will just have to let me go next year," she told herself, thinking how wonderful it would be to soar up into the sky, sweeping down all the cobwebs she could find.

Wendy closed her eyes and pretended that her name would be the next one called. She would step right up and sail off into the sky on her broom. She could just see herself silhouetted against the full moon.

"Hulga Witch, zone 13. Ondora, zone 14." The dispatcher's voice brought Wendy out of her dream with a start. Had she missed any names? She hoped not.

"Wendy, stop your dreaming and keep your mind on your business," said the dispatcher angrily.

Everyone keeps telling me to keep my mind on business. I can't help it if there are so many more interesting things to think about, Wendy thought.

She had just crossed off the last two names and was trying hard to look alert, when one of the witches came limping back. She carried a broken broom in her hands.

"Hagatha! What happened to you?" asked the dispatcher.

"My broom broke! It just up and broke in mid-air and dumped me in that old mill pond," she sobbed. Muddy water dripped off her nose and streamed from her long straggly hair.

"Oh, dear," cried the supervisor, wringing her gnarled hands. "We need every cobweb we can get. They are none too plentiful this year. And there is not another able-bodied witch to take your place."

"I'll go!" cried Wendy without even thinking, jumping up and down as if she were on a pogo stick.

"You?" The supervisor, the dispatcher, and Hagatha all looked down their long crooked noses at her.

"I can do it. I know I can."

"Oh, I don't think so. You are awfully young," said the supervisor.

"It's too big a responsibility," said the dispatcher, shaking her head.

"I promise I'll do a good job. I got 'A' in sky sweeping on my last report."

"But you can't keep your mind on your business," said the dispatcher.

"I will, I will. I promise!"

"As you did when you were mending your cape and sewed it to your dress?" asked Hagatha.

Wendy's face felt hot. That could happen to anyone, she thought.

"Or as you did when you were supposed to be picking out a tail-guard cat and got so interested in watching the kittens play that you forgot all about your afternoon classes?" asked the dispatcher.

"Please let me try," begged Wendy, feeling hot all over.

"Well, there isn't anyone else. Are you sure you can keep your mind on your business and not get lost?" asked the supervisor.

"I'm sure."

"Actually, it's not too big a territory. You might be able to handle it. Do you know the boundaries?"

"Oh, yes. Between Walla Walla and Minnewauken."

"Very well, then, you may go. Now remember. Keep your mind on your business. Don't get lost. And be back before sunup."

"I'll remember," said Wendy. She slung Hagatha's cobweb bag over her shoulder, called her cat, mounted her broom, gave the magic sign, and took off.

At first it was pure fun streaking across the dark sky gathering the silky white cobwebs. Wendy did a good job, too. There wasn't a cobweb left all the way to Ekalaka. But by now she was beginning to get tired. This job was a lot of work, she thought. She checked the time by the moon. It was still high in the sky.

"Good. It's early and I'm nearly half done. I have plenty of time to take a wee bit of a rest and still get home before sunup."

Wendy flew down to a church steeple and sat on it. Her cat stretched out along her shoulders and curled its long tail under her chin.

"Ooooh, this feels good," she said. "If only I'd thought to tuck an apple in my pocket before I left. I'm hungry enough to eat a cat."

"Sssst!" Her cat arched its back.

"Oh, I beg your pardon! I meant a jack-o'-lantern.

"How beautiful everything looks from up here," she said. The bright full moon shining through the trees made lacy patterns on the ground.

"I wonder what all those spooks and goblins are doing running from door to door." Wendy leaned so far over she nearly fell off the steeple.

"I think I'll just dip down there and see."

She forgot all about being tired. She mounted her broom and down she flew.

"Why, those gruesome goblins are getting goodies," she said as she landed near a group who had just rung a doorbell and shouted, "Trick or treat!"

"Can anyone do that?" she asked a little ghost.

"Sure, if you are in costume," he said.

"Costume?" asked Wendy.

"Sure, come on, join us. That's the neatest witch's costume I ever saw."

Before long Wendy was the first to every door and the last to leave. She joined one group after another. She ate every cookie and piece of candy she was given. After a while she was so full she couldn't eat another bite. Then she used her cobweb bag to carry her treats. Soon, even the bag was overflowing. She was having so much fun that she forgot about her cat, the time, and her duties.

Finally, when everyone else had gone home, she remembered and glanced at the moon.

"Oh, look at the time! I'd better get going or I'll never finish." She knew that if she didn't get back by sunup she'd be grounded next year — and if she didn't finish her job and bring back lots of cobwebs the witches wouldn't have enough to last them the whole year. Wendy would be disgraced and the other witches would be terribly angry.

"Come on, Kitty. We'd better go," she said turning to her cat.

"Kitty? Kitty? Where are you?" Now that she thought about it Wendy realized that she hadn't seen her cat for some time.

"Oh, dear, I do hope he isn't lost. I have to find him. I can't leave without my cat."

Wendy mounted her broom, even though she knew it was dangerous to fly so close to earth without a tail guard. But she had to find her cat and her feet hurt too much to walk; they weren't used to sidewalks at all. She gave the magic sign, but nothing happened. She tried again. Still nothing happened.

"What's the matter with my broom? How can I get my sky swept if I can't fly? And if I have to walk home I'll be terribly late." Big tears rolled down her cheeks. "Oh, why did I let my mind get off my business? If I ever find Kitty and get home, I'll never let my mind stray again," she promised herself. She gave the magic sign once more. Still nothing happened.

The only hope was to get off and look for the cat on foot. She limped along, dragging her broom, poking under boxes and barrels.

"Here Kitty, Kitty, here Kitty, Kitty," she called.

The cold crisp air made her fingers tingle.

She tried to go back the way she had come, but she couldn't remember where she had been. It had been so much fun she had forgotten to notice.

"Besides, it's hard to get your bearings down here on the ground. I need to be up in the sky so I can see the lay of the land," she muttered.

She passed the fire house and two churches, but nothing looked familiar. At last she saw a large building at the end of the street. She hurried toward it. "Maybe that is the church with the steeple," she said to herself.

But it was not the church. There was a big sign in front.

"F-A-R-M S-T-A-N-D," she spelled. "I wonder what a farm stand is. It's such an interesting building. Maybe if I just took a peek inside I could .... Oh, no! I mustn't let my mind get off my business again. If I had paid attention before, I wouldn't be in so much trouble now."

So on she went, past the building to the barn behind it. "Here Kitty, Kitty," she called.

Her cat appeared through the open barn door. It purred and rubbed against her leg.

"Oh, Kitty. I thought I had lost you!" She held her cat close. It was dusty, dirty, and smelly, but she didn't care. She felt like crying she was so happy.

"What's all over you? Cobwebs! Where did you get them?"

The cat jumped out of her arms and ran into the barn. Wendy ran after. It was dark inside. At first all Wendy could see was an old horse asleep in a stall. Then she saw hundreds of cobwebs hanging from every beam and rafter. The moon shining through the open doors and windows made them look like tiny fish nets.

"Oh, look at all those beautiful cobwebs," she cried. "If we had them they would last us all year.

"Pardon me, Mr. Horse, but would you mind if I took just a few? Then I won't be letting the witches down even if I am late getting back."

"Naaaay," said the horse, swishing its tail.

"Oh, thank you," Wendy said, then, using her broom, she swept down all the webs she could reach from the floor. She started to put them in her bag, but it was filled to the top with goodies.

"I'll trade you some of my treats for some more of the cobwebs," she said to the horse. It didn't object so she poured half the goodies into a grain bin.

"I wish I could reach those webs up in the loft. I'll try my broom again." Setting her bag on the floor, she got on her broom, said the magic words and, surprisingly, off she went.

"For goodness' sakes!" she exclaimed. She went back down and picked up her bag, but when she got back on her broomstick with it, she couldn't fly.

"My bag is too heavy! It's all that candy and stuff! Well, I'd much rather have those lovely cobwebs than the goodies. Could I trade them all for the rest of the cobwebs?" she asked the horse.

The horse only nodded, which Wendy decided meant yes.

She filled another bin with the rest of the treats and carefully gathered all the webs in the barn.

When she had finished, she picked up her cat and checked the moon for the time. It was well past midnight.

"Goodbye, Mr. Horse, and thanks," she called as she sailed off into the night.

She worked as fast as she could and since there weren't very many webs between Ekalaka and Minnewauken she did manage to finish on time. She returned home just as the sky began to grow pink.

"Here comes Wendy at last," cried the dispatcher.

"Look what a mess she is," said Hagatha. "Her dress is torn and there's dirt on her face. I told you she couldn't do the job."

"But look at that bag full of cobwebs!" exclaimed the supervisor. "It is the fattest bag anyone has brought home tonight."

"You can't have gathered all those webs on my old dry run between Walla Walla and Minnewauken. Where did you ever find them?" asked Hagatha.

But that was Wendy's and Kitty's secret and they weren't telling anybody.

"Well, she said she'd do a good job," said the supervisor, feeling very proud of her smallest witch. "From now on she'll be assigned permanently to that territory."

"I guess she has learned to keep her mind on her business at last," said the dispatcher.

"I sure have." Wendy smiled to herself as she limped away to her bed.